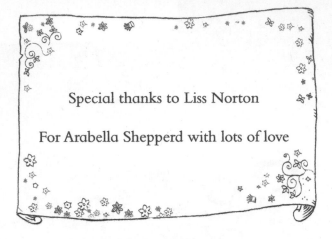

Special thanks to Liss Norton

For Arabella Shepperd with lots of love

ORCHARD BOOKS

First published in Great Britain in 2014 by Orchard Books
This edition published in 2016 by The Watts Publishing Group

5 7 9 10 8 6 4

A CIP catalogue record for this book is available from the British Library.

ISBN 978 1 40832 908 5

Printed in Great Britain by Clays Ltd, St Ives plc

MIX
Paper from
responsible sources
FSC® C104740
www.fsc.org

The paper and board used in this book are made from wood from responsible sources

Orchard Books
An imprint of Hachette Children's Group
Part of The Watts Publishing Group Limited
Carmelite House, 50 Victoria Embankment, London EC4Y 0DZ

An Hachette UK Company
www.hachette.co.uk
www.hachettechildrens.co.uk

Series created by Hothouse Fiction
www.hothousefiction.com

Emerald Unicorn

ROSIE BANKS

ORCHARD

This is the Secret Kingdom

Unicorn Valley

Contents

A Disastrous Discovery!

"Snap!" cried Jasmine Smith. She picked up all the cards and beamed at her best friends, Summer Hammond and Ellie Macdonald. "I win again!"

"Have you got cards hidden up your sleeves?" Ellie asked, giggling. "That's your third win in a row!"

Before Jasmine could reply, there was a huge clap of thunder that rattled Ellie's bedroom window. The girls jumped up and ran to look out. The sky was covered in thick, grey clouds and rain was pouring down. "Yuck!" sighed Summer. "I don't think we're going to be able to play in the garden at all today."

Lightning fizzed across the sky, then more thunder boomed. Ellie shivered.

"Thunder always reminds me of Queen Malice," she said. "I hate hearing it when we're in the Secret Kingdom because it means she's not far away."

"I wonder what she's up to right now," said Jasmine thoughtfully. "Something horrible, I bet!"

The friends shuddered at the thought. They were the only people in the world who knew about the Secret Kingdom, a wonderful land filled with unicorns, mermaids, brownies and other magical creatures. It was ruled by kind King Merry, but his wicked sister, Queen Malice, was always trying to take over. With the help of their pixie friend, Trixi, the girls had defeated Malice lots of times before.

A tingle of excitement ran down

Summer's spine as she thought about the Secret Kingdom. "We haven't been there for ages," she said. "I wish we could go back."

"It does seem a long time since we last heard from Trixi," Jasmine agreed. She took the Magic Box out of her bag and placed it on Ellie's bed. The carved box had a mirror in its lid, surrounded by six green gems.

The girls gathered round the box excitedly, then drew back with gasps of horror.

"What's wrong with it?" cried Ellie.

The carved pictures on the sides of the box had changed. Instead of beautiful unicorns, fairies and mermaids, there were Storm Sprites and huge mean-looking creatures! The green gems looked almost grey and the mirror was completely black. Peering into it was like looking into a bottomless, black pool.

Summer shivered. "This isn't right," she said, gulping down a knot of fear that had risen in her throat. "The box has *never* looked like this before."

"It was OK when I checked it last week," said Jasmine with a frown. "Let's try to open it."

The girls put their hands on the gems on top of the box to see if it would magically open, but nothing happened. Then Jasmine ran her hands along the lid and pulled gently. But it was no good. The box stayed dark and firmly shut.

Summer took Ellie and Jasmine's hands and squeezed them gently. "What if we can't go back to the Secret Kingdom ever again?" she asked in a shocked voice, saying out loud what they were all thinking.

"No, look!" cried Ellie. "Something's happening."

They all held their breath as a faint shimmer crossed the mirror for a moment. It was nothing like the usual brightness that shone out when Trixi had a message for them. As the shimmer faded, a picture started to appear!

"That's never happened before!" Ellie exclaimed. "What is it?"

Gradually the picture got clearer and clearer until the girls could see a familiar face in the blackened mirror.

"King Merry!" Jasmine cried.

"But whatever has happened to him?"

Summer gasped in dismay.

The little king looked very unhappy
and his white hair
and beard hung
in tangles. He
wasn't wearing
his crown and
above his head
was a barred
window that let in
just a little grey light.

"Is he in prison?" asked Summer,
feeling shocked.

"Girls," the king whispered anxiously.
"I hope you get this message. The Secret
Kingdom needs your help! I'm using the
Secret Spellbook to send you this, but I
have to be quick. You MUST use one of
your glitter-dust wishes to call the Secret

Spellbook to you. When it arrives, find a spell that will bring you to me."

The girls exchanged anxious looks. The Secret Spellbook contained old, powerful magic and was only ever used by the ruler of the Secret Kingdom. Things must be very bad indeed if King Merry wanted *them* to use the spellbook!

"Trixi can't come and get you this time," King Merry continued. "Keep watching and the Magic Box will show you everything. But you MUST call the spellbook to you as soon as you can. Oh dearie, dearie me!"

Suddenly the picture of King Merry vanished and his wicked sister, Queen Malice, appeared in the mirror of the Magic Box.

As the girls watched, horrified, she

picked up King Merry's crown from
a golden table and placed it on her
own head. "Now *I* rule the Secret
Kingdom!" she cackled. She snatched up
her thunderbolt staff and sent lightning
streaking around the room.

"Isn't that King Merry's throne room?"
asked Summer.

"I think so," gasped Ellie.

"Or it used to be," Jasmine said
anxiously. As they watched, mud
and slime began to ooze across the
marble floor and the curtains changed
from King Merry's royal purple to a
horrid black. Cobwebs fell down from
the ceiling and the cheerful portraits
of King Merry changed into sneering
pictures of the queen!

Queen Malice's Storm Sprites, nasty

creatures with bat-like wings, came
swooping down from the ceiling. They
flew around the queen, cheering, as
she stalked to King Merry's throne
and sat down.

"What are *those* things?" asked Jasmine as several huge lumpy creatures lumbered into view. They had thick, stumpy legs and long arms that reached to their knees. Their heads, which were the size of boulders, were dotted with clumps of bristly, green hair. They bowed to the wicked queen. "Welcome, troll friends," she said.

"Trolls!" Ellie whispered. "How could she let such horrible creatures into the palace?"

Suddenly, the picture faded and the girls looked at one another in dismay. "She's done it at last," said Summer in a shocked voice. "Queen Malice is the ruler of the Secret Kingdom!"

The Secret Spellbook

"We have to help King Merry!" cried
Jasmine determinedly.

The girls turned to the box and the
dark lid slowly creaked open with a noise
like a sad sigh. Ellie held out her hand
and caught the bag of glitter dust, a gift
from the fairies of Glitter Beach, and the
magic map, as they both floated up into
the air. There was enough glitter dust to
grant two wishes. Ellie unfolded the map
and spread it out on the bed.

"Oh no!" gasped Summer. Normally the map showed all the lovely places and creatures of the Secret Kingdom, but today everything looked dark, gloomy and spooky.

"Look at King Merry's palace," gasped Jasmine. The Enchanted Palace was usually pink and sparkling. Now it looked dark and scary, with ugly gargoyles, who looked a bit like Storm Sprites, perched on the turrets.

"That's new," said Summer, pointing to a spiky bridge at the top of the map. "Look, it leads to an island."

They all peered closer, trying to read the words written next to the island in tiny letters.

"Troll Territories!" gasped Ellie. "That must be where the trolls are from."

"We've got to get to the Secret Kingdom and find Trixi," Jasmine said. "She'll know what we need to do."

Ellie made sure that the door to her bedroom was closed and then rushed back to join Summer and Jasmine.

"Here goes!" said Jasmine. She took a pinch of the glitter dust and

threw it up into the air.

The girls held hands and chanted, "We wish for the Secret Spellbook!"

The room darkened a little, then a shimmer of golden light began to glow in the middle of the floor. With a sudden flash, there it was — a magnificent leather-covered book with glittering, curly shapes on the front.

Jasmine's breath caught as she opened the cover. A few specks of golden dust floated up. "We've never used this before, so we'll have to be very careful and make sure we pick the right spell to take us to King Merry," she said.

The girls went through the book, turning the ancient pages carefully so that they didn't damage them.

"What if something goes wrong?" asked Summer nervously. "We could end up somewhere dangerous...or accidentally get separated!"

Jasmine squeezed Summer's hand. "I know, but we have to help King Merry, and this is our only way of reaching the Secret Kingdom without Trixi!"

"You're right," said Summer determinedly. "We need to be brave!"

"How about this one?" asked Ellie, flicking through the book. "A travelling spell."

They read the spell quickly. "It's perfect," said Jasmine.

The girls stood and picked up the

spellbook. Ellie quickly grabbed her backpack from the back of her door to carry the spellbook in when they got to the Secret Kingdom.

The friends linked arms and held onto the book tightly, keeping it open at the right page.

"Here goes!" said Summer, her voice shaking nervously.

"Let's read the spell together," said Ellie. "And say 'Secret Kingdom' in the third line. Ready?"

"Ready," said Jasmine softly.

The three friends looked at each other. They could hardly believe they were about to use a magic spell to transport themselves to the Secret Kingdom!

Ellie slowly counted to three and together they chanted the magic words:

"Ancient magic, take us swiftly
Far away through time and space.
Carry us to the Secret Kingdom
And set us in a helpful place."

The spellbook began to shimmer more brightly until the whole of Ellie's bedroom seemed to be made of gold. Then the girls felt themselves rising up in the air. The friends held the spellbook tightly as they whizzed round. Just a few moments later, they landed with a gentle bump.

As the sparkles cleared, they saw that they were in a long corridor. Flaming torches blazed in brackets fixed to the wall, and by their flickering light they saw a row of open doors and a closed one with a barred window.

"Where are we?" asked Summer, glancing around nervously.

"I think we're in Thunder Castle,

down in the dungeons," said Jasmine in a worried voice. "We've been here before on one of our other adventures."

"The spell said it was taking us to a 'helpful place'," said Ellie. "Maybe King Merry is here?"

Jasmine took down the nearest torch and they tiptoed down the corridor.

Ellie put her hand to her head and smiled. "At least we still have our special tiaras," she said, feeling something resting on top of her head. Then she looked at Jasmine and Summer more carefully. "Oh no!" she cried. "They don't look right at all!"

The three friends took off their tiaras – which showed they were Very Important Friends of King Merry's – and looked at them in dismay. Normally they were

sparkly but now each one looked grubby
and dull.

Summer sighed sadly. "We *have* to
find King Merry and see what's going
on!" The girls continued checking each
dungeon. When they came to the closed
door, they peered through the barred
window. King Merry was sitting on
the stone floor, staring into a muddy
puddle. He was dressed
in stripy prison
clothes and
there was
a ball and
chain fastened
around his
ankle.

"King Merry!"
cried Ellie.

The little king looked up, startled, then his gaze fell on the girls and his face broke into a relieved smile. "Crowns and sceptres, thank goodness you're here!" he cried. He scrambled to his feet, then tripped over the ball and chain. "Botheration!" he exclaimed, jumping up again. He picked up the ball and staggered to the door with it. "Did my message work? It took a very complicated spell to make a link between the mirror of the Magic Box and that puddle over there," he said, proudly.

"It worked," said Ellie with a grin. "And now we've come to help."

"How did Queen Malice take over the kingdom?" asked Jasmine.

"And where's Trixi?" added Summer.

"Well, it's a very sad story," said the

little king, shaking his head forlornly. "Trixi and I were travelling by royal swan a couple of days ago when we found ourselves surrounded by thick storm clouds. We had to make an emergency landing and suddenly my sister's Storm Sprites and lots of horrible trolls grabbed us."

"Couldn't Trixi's magic stop them?"
asked Ellie.

King Merry shook his head sadly.
"There were too many."

"We saw a new bridge on the map
between the Secret Kingdom and the
Troll Territories," said Jasmine. "That
must be how the trolls came in to the
kingdom."

"Malice did a deal with them," King
Merry explained. "She offered them part
of the kingdom if they helped her steal
my throne. Then she banished me to this
dungeon and took the crown for herself!"

"And what about Trixi?" asked
Summer.

A tear trickled down King Merry's
cheek. "That's the worst part of all!
Poor Trixi has to work for Malice. As a

royal pixie she must obey the ruler of the Secret Kingdom, no matter who it is."

The girls looked at one another in horror.

"We've *got* to stop Queen Malice and rescue you and Trixi," said Jasmine.

"We've defeated the queen before," Summer said. "I'm sure we can do it again. Don't worry, King Merry. We *will* find a way of making you king again!"

Ancient Magic

King Merry dried his eyes. "Thank you so much, girls. The good news is that I can help you to help me!" He looked puzzled for a moment. "Or should that be, 'I can help me to help you?' No, no that's not right... Anyway, all you need to do is find the four royal jewels from my old crown and then a new crown will be magically formed," said the king happily.

"But there weren't any jewels in your old crown, were there?" Ellie asked, feeling puzzled.

"They were on the inside to keep them safe," the king explained. "An emerald, a sapphire, a ruby and a diamond."

"So where are the royal jewels now?" asked Summer, "Aren't they still inside the crown?"

"That's just it," King Merry said. "I used the Secret Spellbook to put a spell on my crown to stop Malice from taking it."

"But Queen Malice *has* taken it." Jasmine frowned.

King Merry looked a bit sheepish. "Yes, well…er, the magic *sort of* worked! My sister took the crown, but the royal jewels disappeared, and without them she will never be the *true* ruler of the kingdom."

The girls smiled at each other. Poor King Merry's spells and inventions always went a bit wonky!

"So where are the royal jewels now?" asked Summer.

"That's the problem," King Merry said sadly. "Because the spell didn't work *quite* as I'd planned, I don't know where the jewels have ended up."

"At least you stopped Queen Malice getting them," Summer said, squeezing King Merry's hand through the bars of the cell.

"That's right," agreed Ellie. "And now we've got the chance to find the jewels without her even knowing we're here."

King Merry cheered up. "I knew you'd

be able to set things right! Once you've found all the royal jewels, a new crown will be created by magic, and I'll rule the kingdom again!"

Suddenly there was a loud bang. The girls jumped in surprise.

"What was that?" gasped Summer.

"It sounded like a door slamming," Jasmine said.

"I can hear footsteps," Ellie said anxiously. "But they sound a long way away."

"It's the Storm Sprites," said King Merry. "They come and check on me now and then. I wish I could get out. That would give the silly things a shock!"

"Why don't we use the Secret Spellbook to magic you out?" suggested

Summer. "The spell we used to come here worked perfectly. I'm sure we could find one to help you." She hurriedly flipped through the pages of the old book, searching for the right spell. "Here!" she cried. "An escaping spell!"

The girls quickly chanted the words together:

"Ancient magic, break these bars
And then unlock the door.
Free the king from his ball and chain,
Imprison him no more."

A whirlwind of violet light whooshed out of the spellbook and into the cell. It curled around the window bars and puffed through the keyhole.

The girls watched eagerly, waiting for the chain and bars to break, and for the door to fly open. But nothing happened.

"There must be an enchantment on the cell!" Jasmine said.

"Don't worry about me," said King Merry with a brave sigh. "Finding the jewels is the most important thing. Leave me here while you go and get them all!"

"If we can't get you out," Ellie said to the little king, "maybe we can magic things in."

"How will that help?" asked Jasmine, puzzled.

Ellie looked over Summer's shoulder as she turned the spellbook pages. "There!" she exclaimed. "A comfort spell! That should do the trick!" She quickly read it out:

"Ancient magic, make this room
As comfy as can be.
Bring things from King Merry's home
To keep him company!"

There was a blinding flash and
suddenly the cell was decorated just
like King Merry's bedroom back in the
Enchanted Palace! He had a grand
four-poster bed with a purple, velvet
bedspread, an armchair and footstool
embroidered with gold crowns and a
thick carpet covering the stone floor.
On a little table sat a covered silver dish.
When the king lifted the lid there was a
delicious roast dinner underneath!

"Thank you!" cried King Merry. "I'll
be happy to wait here now until you get
back." He sank into the armchair with a

relieved sigh. Even though the ball and
chain were still around his ankle,
he looked much more comfortable!

Suddenly they heard the footsteps
again. They were getting louder and
were accompanied by the squabbling
sound of Storm Sprite voices.

"Quick!" whispered Summer. "We
have to hide!"

"How will we know where to look for the royal jewels, King Merry?" Jasmine asked urgently.

"Use the Secret Spellbook. It has a finding spell that will search the kingdom for them. Then it will transport you to where the jewel is hidden." he explained.

The footsteps echoed along the corridor.

"In here," hissed Summer. She pulled Ellie and Jasmine into one of the empty cells.

"I'll look for the spell right away," whispered Summer. She turned the pages of the spellbook slowly so they wouldn't rustle.

Two Storm Sprites stomped past. The girls heard them stop outside King Merry's cell. "Where's all this stuff come

from?" one of them asked.

"How should I know?" replied the other.

"Listen, big nose," snapped the first. "When I ask a question I expect a proper answer."

As the sprites bickered, Summer sped through the spellbook. "Got it!" she whispered. "A finding spell."

The girls looked at the spell, which was written in delicate, sloping handwriting on the yellowed pages. As they watched, two more lines appeared and suddenly the spell was complete:

Something's lost that must be found,
Search through sea, air and ground...
You must find the jewel that's green,
Where horned creatures can be seen.

"A jewel that's green," said Jasmine. "Well, that must be the emerald!"

"And 'horned creatures' are unicorns!" cried Summer. "I think we need to go to Unicorn Valley!"

Summer clutched the book and Jasmine and Ellie put their arms around her. Together they read out the spell.

Immediately a whirlwind of coloured sparkles shot out of the spellbook. They were off to Unicorn Valley!

Unicorn Valley

Once they were outside Thunder Castle the whirlwind slowed and they spun gently, looking down at the Secret Kingdom. Dark thunderclouds hung low over the land, blotting out the sun and spreading spooky shadows everywhere.

"It looks awful," said Summer with a shiver. "It just doesn't seem like the Secret Kingdom at all."

A lightning bolt zigzagged out of a cloud and hit the ground, sending sparks flying up. The girls could see burn marks in the grass.

"This is terrible," groaned Ellie, peeking out between her fingers. She always hated flying and this flight was upsetting *and* scary. She didn't even know how they were staying up in the air!

They floated over Magic Mountain. "Look at the poor snow brownies," gasped Jasmine. They were desperately trying to make ice sculptures, but the ice had melted into piles of useless grey slush.

Soon they came to Glitter Beach, but the beautiful sand was black and lumpy. A group of fairies flew by below them, chased by jeering Storm Sprites.

"We've got to fix all this," Ellie said with tears in her eyes.

"We will," said Jasmine fiercely. "Finding the emerald will be the first step to putting everything right."

They saw hills ahead and a moment later they were lowered gently into a valley. Ellie took the Secret Spellbook and held onto it tightly.

"Is this really Unicorn Valley?" Jasmine gasped as she stared round. The beautiful flower-filled fields and emerald-green lawns were gone, and the girls could see nothing but black, gloopy mud in every direction. The trees that shaded the valley had been cut down, leaving ugly, jagged stumps.

"Where are our unicorn friends?" whispered Summer, feeling close to tears.

Ellie hugged her. "It'll be OK," she said. "We'll find the unicorns and put everything back to normal."

"And what's that awful smell?" Jasmine said, holding her nose. "It's like rotten cabbage!"

"I don't know," said Summer. "But let's look for Littlehorn and the other unicorns. They might know what's going on."

They hadn't gone far before they heard growly, grumbly voices ahead.

The girls hid behind a rock as four huge trolls appeared. They were easily three times as tall as the girls, with hunched backs and massive heads. One of them was carrying a large glass bottle half full of a sparkling, glittery golden mist.

"Careful with that!" shouted a voice. A Storm Sprite swooped down from the clouds and flapped around the trolls' heads. "The bottle keeps those annoying unicorns under control."

The trolls stopped walking and held the bottle up in the air. They peered at the glitter inside dopily, scratching their huge heads and frowning. "But there's no unicorns in it," one said in a slow, gravelly voice. "Just silly sparkly stuff."

The sprite laughed nastily. "Of course there are no unicorns *in* the bottle, durr-brains! We've *shown* you how to use it. When the unicorns swish their horns around, just take the stopper out."

The trolls immediately pulled the stopper out of the bottle and Ellie felt the Secret Spellbook jerk in her hands. She opened it hurriedly, wondering what was going on. Glittery magic streamed out of it. She quickly slammed the book shut again.

"Not now, you nitwits!" screeched the

Storm Sprite bossily.

Jasmine couldn't help giggling. Queen Malice's trolls were even sillier than the Storm Sprites!

The trolls put the stopper back into the bottle.

"Now, go and check that the unicorns are working," said the Storm Sprite, flying away and muttering to himself about the silly trolls.

The trolls trudged on. "I hope them unicorns are planting lots of stinky sprouts," said one.

"Stinky sprouts! Yummy!" exclaimed another, happily.

"That must be what that awful smell is," whispered Jasmine.

"Let's follow the trolls," said Ellie quietly. "It sounds as though they'll lead us to the unicorns. And we have to find out *exactly* what that bottle is doing!"

Hearts thumping, the girls crept out from behind the rock and tiptoed after the trolls. They could hardly bear to look. It was terrible to see gloopy black mud where flowers and trees had once grown.

Soon they came to a massive field planted with tall purple plants. The smell was even worse here.

"These must be stinky sprouts," said Summer. "Ugh, how could anyone bear to eat anything this pongy?"

"Look! There's a unicorn," Jasmine gasped. "And there's another one over there!" They watched as the beautiful creatures worked their way dejectedly between the rows of sprouts, digging out weeds with their horns.

"The poor things are being forced

to dig up their beautiful land to plant disgusting sprouts," said Ellie in dismay.

Jasmine squared her shoulders. "We've *got* to find that emerald and stop this. Come on!"

Missing Magic

"There's Littlehorn!" whispered Summer excitedly as the girls crept along the edge of the field. Littlehorn was the daughter of Silvertail, the unicorns' leader.

Checking that no trolls were watching them, the girls ducked in amongst the stinky sprouts. They covered their noses and crouched down, so they were hidden by the plants as they darted over to speak to the little unicorn.

Littlehorn was digging stones out of the
soil with her hooves, but she looked up at
the sound of the girls' footsteps. The girls
were shocked to see the change in her. Her
beautiful white coat and pink mane were
streaked with mud and she looked very sad.
But her blue eyes brightened a little when
she saw them.

"Summer, Ellie, Jasmine!" she whinnied.

Summer stroked her soft coat and the little
unicorn nuzzled against her.

"It's lovely to see you, Littlehorn,"
Summer said.

"I'm very glad you're all here,"
said Littlehorn. "Do you think you
can help us?"

Before the girls could reply and ask
Littlehorn about the emerald, a loud hooter
sounded, making them jump.

"What was that?" gasped Ellie.

"It's the trolls' lunchtime alarm," Littlehorn said. "They eat hundreds of sprouts, then have a nap. But we have to keep on working." She stamped her hoof crossly.

The girls watched the trolls move to the far end of the field where a lone tree stood. There was a huge tub of sprouts beneath it. The greedy trolls sat down in the shade and began scoffing the

sprouts, chomping and burping loudly.

"Poor Littlehorn," sighed Summer as the little unicorn began to dig out weeds.

"Look, there's Silvertail," said Ellie, pointing down the field.

The girls crept quickly towards  the majestic unicorn. Her silver mane and tail were dirty and her hooves were caked in mud. Her golden horn was shockingly dull.

"Silvertail," Jasmine called in a low voice. "Over here!"

The unicorn looked up and whinnied hello. "Girls," she smiled. "Thank goodness you're here."

The girls crept over to her.

"I'd better keep working," said Silvertail. "The horrible trolls are too lazy to plant their own disgusting plants and are making us do it instead!" She dug out a stone from the ground with her hoof, picked it up in her mouth and dropped it into a bucket.

"Why are you working for the trolls?" Jasmine asked. "Can't you use your magic to get rid of them?"

"We've tried," sighed Silvertail, "but it won't work. It's as though something's stealing our magic. Every time we try to use the magic from our horns it seems to zoom away!"

"The bottle!" gasped Ellie.

Silvertail stared at her.

"The trolls have a big bottle with some glittery stuff inside it," Ellie continued excitedly. "When they took the cork out of the bottle earlier, the spellbook started to behave very strangely, as if the magic was being sucked out of it! *And* the sprites talked about using it to keep the unicorns under control."

"You're right!" cried Jasmine.

"The sprite said the trolls should take the stopper out when the unicorns waved their horns about," Summer remembered with a gasp. "And the unicorns make magic with their horns. Taking away their magic would stop them from standing up to the trolls."

They looked over at the trolls. A few were still eating, their cheeks bulging with sprouts, but most of them had already fallen asleep and were snoring loudly.

"Where's the one who had the bottle?" asked Ellie.

"There," said Summer, pointing to a large troll sleeping under a tree. "But what's he done with it?" The troll was fast asleep, but there was no sign of the bottle anywhere.

"I can see it," said Jasmine suddenly. The troll had wedged it high up into the branches of the tree. The stopper had been knocked half out of the bottle.
Ellie squeezed the Secret Spellbook's cover tightly. She wanted to make sure that no magic would be sucked out of it!

"What if we're wrong about the bottle taking the magic?" Summer said cautiously. "Shouldn't we start looking for the emerald instead?"

"The emerald?" said Silvertail, pricking up her ears as she looked at the girls.

Jasmine quickly explained about the missing royal jewels.

Littlehorn crept closer to listen to the girls, too. She flicked her tail crossly. "If only we could get rid of the horrid trolls, we could help you find it!"

"Let's work out what's going on with your missing magic first," said Jasmine determinedly. "Once you have your magic back, it'll be much easier for you to help us look for the jewel."

"Very well," said Silvertail. "I'll use some magic and let's see what happens."

The brave unicorn pointed her horn at
the trolls and a stream of sparkling magic
poured out. It wound across the field
like a golden ribbon, then disappeared
into the bottle, leaving Silvertail's horn a
horrible grey colour. Littlehorn whinnied

sadly and gently rubbed her head against her mother.

Silvertail shivered. "That proves it!" she said. "Our missing magic is inside that bottle!"

An Unwelcome Visitor!

"We need to get the unicorns' magic out of that bottle!" Jasmine said fiercely. "But how?"

"We can't use the spellbook," Ellie said thoughtfully, "because the bottle will steal its magic too."

"If only Trixi was here," groaned Summer. "She'd know what to do."

The girls fell silent. They all really missed their pixie friend.

A magnificent unicorn came over, keeping a careful eye on the trolls. He had a beautiful emerald-green coat and a long golden mane and tail. "My name is Greenhoof," he said, bowing his head in greeting. "I overheard what you were saying about the bottle and I have a suggestion. Why don't we smash it?"

"That's a good idea!" smiled Jasmine. "If we break the bottle, all the magic inside it will escape!"

"Let's distract the trolls so they move away from the bottle," Summer suggested. "Then we can grab the bottle and destroy it."

"Great," said Ellie, bending down and picking a stinky sprout from its stalk. "And we can use these horrible things to wake up the lazy creatures!"

The girls picked as many of the horrid stinky sprouts as they could and stuffed them in their pockets. Then they crept forwards

towards the sleeping trolls and hid behind the tree.

"Wake up, you big lumps!" shouted Jasmine rudely, aiming a sprout at a particularly huge troll.

"Take that!" cried Summer, sending two stinky sprouts flying through the air at the same time, hitting a nearby troll on the nose *and* on the ear with two big green SPLATS!

With rumbles and grumbles, the lazy trolls started to wake up, and the girls ducked out of sight behind the tree trunk.

"Over here!" Littlehorn and Greenhoof yelled at the trolls as they galloped around them, their hooves kicking mud and stinky-sprout plants up into the air.

The trolls got up on their huge flat feet and ran after the unicorns, leaving the bottle in the tree behind them!

At a nod of Silvertail's head, the unicorns galloped off, leading the trolls away.

"Well done, unicorns," Jasmine said under her breath. "Now, let's get that bottle!"

The girls could see the bottle in the tree, filled with glittering magic, but it was very high up in the branches.

"Jasmine, you're really good at balancing," said Summer. "If we helped you up, could you swing onto that first branch, and then climb up and grab the bottle?"

"I think so," said Jasmine. "Good idea!"

Summer and Ellie laced their hands together and lifted Jasmine up as far as they could so that she could grab the

lowest branch
with her hands.
She quickly swung
herself onto the first
branch and then
clambered up
to where the
bottle was
resting.

As Jasmine
climbed,
Summer glanced
over at the trolls,
but luckily the
unicorns were doing a good job of
keeping them distracted.

But just as Jasmine's fingertips touched
the bottle, there was a loud shout from
behind them.

"It's those interfering human girls!" a group of Storm Sprites screeched as they came zooming out of the clouds. "And they're trying to get the bottle!"

Jasmine turned around to see where the voices were coming from, but as she did, her foot slipped off the branch!

Summer and Ellie gasped as their friend fell.

"Agh!" Jasmine cried out as she dangled in the air, clinging tightly to the branch with both hands.

"Jasmine!" Summer cried. As she and Ellie looked up at their friend in dismay, a cold wind howled around them, making them shiver. The already grey sky seemed to darken, and a hideous cackle filled the air.

Just when they thought things couldn't

get any worse — it was Queen Malice!

The horrid queen was standing in a shining black coach pulled by six giant black crows. Her Storm Sprites flapped up to meet her.

Landing right by the tree, the queen stepped out of the carriage. Smiling nastily, she stroked King Merry's gold crown, which was resting on her frizzy black hair, and stalked towards the girls. "What are you pesky girls doing here?" she sneered. "Haven't you realised that *I* rule the Secret Kingdom now?"

A Golden Chain

The cruel queen sneered at the girls and then looked around with a frown. "You stupid trolls!" she shrieked. "While you've been running around with the unicorns, these girls almost stole my bottle!"

The trolls clomped over to the tree, looking sheepish.

"I can't hang on for much longer!" Jasmine cried from up in the tree.

Silvertail galloped over. "Let go of the branch, Jasmine!" she called. "I'll catch you on my back."

Jasmine let go. Summer and Ellie held their breath as their friend dropped down lightly onto Silvertail's broad back, but she landed safely with her knees bent like a proper acrobat.

"Are you OK?" Summer whispered.

"Yes, but I didn't get the bottle," said Jasmine sadly.

"No, you didn't," Queen Malice

gave a wicked laugh
and thumped her
thunderbolt staff
on the floor. The
bottle floated
out of the tree,
landing at her
feet. "This belongs
to me, and the
unicorns' magic
will make me even
more powerful!"

The girls exchanged
dismayed glances.

Queen Malice poked
the bottle with her staff
and glared at the unicorns. "Is that all?"
she sneered, looking at the magical mist
inside. "Well, there isn't much in here."

She turned back to look at the unicorns with narrowed eyes. "Do you have any more magic for your queen?" she sneered.

With an angry snort, Littlehorn galloped forwards. The girls had never seen the little unicorn look so cross! "You'll never be our queen!" she shouted bravely. "Now that Summer, Ellie and Jasmine are here they'll get our magic back *and* find the royal emerald!"

The queen frowned at Littlehorn.
"Find the royal emerald? What are you
talking about? All of the royal jewels are
right here, in MY crown!" Queen Malice
took the crown from her messy hair and
peered closely at it. Then, as the girls
watched, her face turned red with anger.
"The jewels aren't here!" she shrieked.
"Where are they? You horrible, sneaky
girls – those jewels belong to me!"

Ellie, Summer and Jasmine stepped
forwards. Summer stroked Littlehorn's
nose softly. The poor little unicorn
looked very upset that she had
accidentally revealed why the girls were
in the kingdom!

"We're going to find the jewels and
make a new crown for the king," cried
Ellie bravely. "King Merry is the true

ruler of the Secret Kingdom!"

As the unicorns cheered defiantly, Greenhoof galloped forwards, heading straight towards the bottle full of glittery magic.

"Go, Greenhoof!' Jasmine cheered as the big unicorn raced to the bottle, ready to smash it with his hooves. But at the last moment, Queen Malice banged her thunderbolt staff on the floor and the bottle shot up into the air and hovered out of reach.

"How dare you try to break my bottle?" shouted the queen. "You'll pay for that!"

She snapped her long fingers and one of her sprites stepped forward. He was holding a floating golden chain which looked like an animal lead. He passed it to the queen and, cackling with cruel laughter, she yanked the chain.

The girls gasped as they saw a flying leaf attached to the end of the floating chain. Kneeling on it was a pixie with a tangle of blonde hair. Trixi!

"Girls! I'm so happy to see you all!" cried Trixi, scrambling to her feet.

The girls ran towards her, but Queen Malice yanked her out of reach. "Stay back!" she warned.

"Are you all right, Trixi?" Summer

called out anxiously.

The little pixie nodded miserably.

Queen Malice shook the golden chain and gave a wicked smile. "Now, show these girls that you serve me, this instant," she commanded. "Tap that silly pixie ring of yours and shrink that disobedient green unicorn! I'll show these unicorns who's the boss around here!"

Trixi glared at the queen furiously, but she had to obey her. She tapped the ring and muttered:

"Pixie magic, hear my call,
And make this unicorn teensy-small."

Pink sparkles came whooshing out of the ring and fizzed around Greenhoof. He immediately shrank to the size of

a cat! The tiny unicorn darted under a stinky sprout plant. The girls were very relieved to see that clever Greenhoof was staying out of reach of the trolls and sprites.

The queen turned back to the girls and narrowed her eyes. "Tell me where the jewels are, or this pixie will shrink ALL your unicorn friends!"

Jasmine stepped forwards. She was just about to say that they had no idea where the jewels were when a thought flashed into her mind. *If Queen Malice thinks we know where the jewels are, we might be able to trick her into releasing the unicorns' magic from the bottle!*

Ridiculous Riddles!

"Um…we know that one of the jewels is close by, but the magic riddles that tell us where to look for it are too hard for us to solve," Jasmine said, thinking on her feet and nudging Ellie and Summer to let them know she had a plan.

"What are these magic riddles?" asked Queen Malice, narrowing her eyes. "I'll work them out myself. Tell me!"

Jasmine looked helplessly at Summer and Ellie. Of course, there weren't really any magic riddles telling them where the jewel was. And now she had to try to think of some!

Summer stepped forward. She winked at Jasmine and said, "Please don't harm our friends, Queen Malice! We'll tell you what we know. Here's the first riddle:

"In Unicorn Valley a sprout's stem
And moonlit trail will hide a gem."

The queen looked round in confusion. "There are hundreds of stinky sprouts," she complained. "And what does it mean by a moonlit trail?"

"We don't know," said Jasmine. "Maybe the hidden jewel can only be found at night?"

"I'm not waiting until it gets dark," snapped the queen. She raised her voice and called to the sprites and trolls. "Search the stem of every stinky sprout to find MY missing jewels."

"There's another riddle," said Jasmine. "And this is the hardest one of all!"

"To reveal the royal jewel,
You must not be a fool!
The trapped magic must be poured,
From the bottle where it's stored."

Queen Malice pointed at the bottle with a triumphant shriek. "It must mean this magic! Well, there's hardly anything in here anyway. It's no good to me. And I need that emerald more!"

She tapped her thunderbolt staff on
the ground and the stopper on top of
the bottle came flying off. Immediately
the unicorns' magic whooshed into the
air in a flurry of sparkles
and glitter.
It rushed
around
Unicorn
Valley,
turning
the air pink and
purple. Finally,
it spiralled to the
tips of the unicorns'
horns, turning them
a brilliant gold once
again.

Trixi jumped up

and down delightedly on her leaf as the unicorns formed a circle around Queen Malice.

"But...but the jewel!" she shrieked. "Where is the jewel? You horrible girls, you tricked me with those riddles!"

"Yes, we did!" cried Summer, laughing in delight.

"Unicorns, be quick, use your magic to send this false ruler away!" cried Silvertail.

Glittering magic flowed from the unicorns' horns. Before Queen Malice could raise her staff, a sparkling white cloud appeared, surrounding the queen, Trixi, and the trolls and sprites. It picked them up, then whizzed them away across the sky at great speed.

The girls heard Queen Malice screeching,

"I'll be back and I will find ALL of those jewels. You won't fool me again!"

Ellie, Jasmine and Summer laughed. "Thank goodness she's gone," said Ellie, then her face fell. "But poor Trixi! Imagine having to work for Queen Malice!"

"We'll find a way to set her free," Jasmine said. "And King Merry too."

"First we need to help Greenhoof," said Summer. The tiny unicorn came out of his hiding place amongst the stinky sprout plants and Summer gently stroked his shimmering green mane.

"Let's find a spell in the Secret
Spellbook to turn him back to his usual
size," said Ellie. She flipped through the
pages. "Here we are, a size spell."

The girls read the spell together:

"Ancient magic, work your spell
So things made big go small,
And all things shrunk by magic words
Return to being tall."

Golden light shone from the Secret
Spellbook. It surrounded Greenhorn and
he grew back to his normal size.

"Thank you, girls," he said, nuzzling
each of them in turn with his nose.

"We can't thank you enough for
helping us to get our magic back!"
said Silvertail. "But we still need to help

you find the emerald."

"Yes," Summer sighed. "Where shall
we start looking?"

Silvertail whinnied loudly and the herd
of unicorns gathered around her. "Now
that our magic has been returned to us,
let's use our powers to help Summer,
Ellie and Jasmine search for the jewel."

Lowering her voice, the unicorn leader
chanted a magical verse:

"Harnessing our unicorn power,
Search each tree and rock and flower.
Let us find the special gem
And give it to our human friends!"

Immediately all of the unicorns' horns
started to glow. Glittery magic flowed
from their horns and poured across the

ground. It travelled up each tree and
every flower and rock, and whatever it
touched became beautiful again. The
unicorns spread out and began to search
the valley, kicking their hooves in the air
and swishing their tails excitedly.

The girls began to search too, delighted to see that their unicorn friends were so happy now that their magic had been returned to them!

A few minutes later, Littlehorn gave a cry. "Summer, Ellie, Jasmine, come and look at this!"

The girls quickly ran over to join Littlehorn. All the streams of magic had joined together and were swirling around one small area of earth in a whirlwind shape.

"But there's nothing there," said Jasmine, disappointed.

"It looks like the ground was disturbed when the stinky sprouts were planted," said Ellie, peering at the ground.

"Our magic is definitely showing something special here," said Silvertail, trotting over to join the girls.

Summer, Ellie and Jasmine started to dig in the ground with their hands. Soon they had made quite a large hole and as they dug deeper, the soft earth seemed to get warmer. After a few moments a magical green glow appeared and together the three girls pulled out a beautiful crescent-shaped green gem!

"The emerald," breathed Summer.

"It's amazing," Jasmine gasped, looking closely at the shimmering jewel. She passed it to Ellie.

"It feels warm," said Ellie. "And sort of special." She dusted it down and put it in the pocket of her jeans. "Thank you for all your help," she said to the unicorns.

The majestic creatures bowed their heads and the magic returned to their horns. "Now the trolls and the Storm Sprites have gone, we can use our magic to get rid of all these stinky sprouts." Silvertail whinnied.

They heard a chirrup overhead and looked up. Three tiny bluebirds

were circling above them. "Those are
the first birds we've seen since we got
here!" exclaimed Ellie. "That has to be
a good sign!" She squeezed Jasmine and
Summer's hands. "Now, let's go and tell
King Merry we've found the first jewel!"

Home Again

The girls hugged their unicorn friends
and then used the Secret Spellbook to
get back to King Merry. He was dozing
in his comfy armchair when the magic
carried the girls to his cell door. He
looked up eagerly as they appeared, then
crossed to his cell door, dragging his ball
and chain behind him.

"Welcome back, my dears, how did you get on?" he asked hopefully.

Ellie took the sparkling emerald out of her pocket and held it out to him.

His face broke into a wide beaming smile. "Oh, well done!" As he took the jewel it began to sparkle more brightly than ever, lightening the gloom.

The girls were pleased to see the little king looking so much more cheerful.

He was almost like his old self again.

"We've got more good news, too," said Summer. "We've seen Trixi! She looked very fed up, but she seems OK. We'll try to get you back together soon!"

King Merry smiled. "Knowing you girls are helping us makes me feel a squillion times better!"

"Let's go and look for the second jewel right away," Ellie suggested. She opened the spellbook to the finding spell and said, "Please help us find the next missing jewel!" The pages of the book rustled quietly but only the first two lines of the spell appeared:

Something's lost that must be found,
Search through sea, air and ground...

"Where's the rest of it?" asked Jasmine.

"Don't worry," said King Merry. "I don't think the spell will be complete until the book's magic has discovered where in the kingdom the second jewel is hidden, and I don't know how long that will take. Once it knows, I'm sure the complete spell will appear in the book." He held out the emerald. "You must keep this in the Other Realm. There's no way my sister will find it there."

Ellie put the jewel back in her pocket. "Are you sure you'll be all right if we go home now, King Merry?" she asked.

"I'll be as rug as a snug in a bug," he said, looking at his comfy bed and armchair. "No, I mean as bug as a rug in a snug." He shook his head and smiled at the girls. "I'll be fine."

"We'll be back soon," promised Summer.

Jasmine found a going-home spell and they linked arms, holding the spellbook between them. "Goodbye, King Merry!" they called. Then they chanted the spell:

"Our quest's complete,
Our journey's done.
Take us home: three, two, one!"

Light streamed out of the Secret Spellbook. It grew brighter and brighter and the girls closed their eyes in surprise. When they opened them again, they were back in Ellie's bedroom.

Jasmine picked up the map of the Secret Kingdom that they'd left on Ellie's bed. "Unicorn Valley is back to normal now," she said happily. The black clouds had rolled back from the valley and they could see grass, flowers and trees again.

"I wonder where the other three jewels are," said Summer softly.

"And which of our friends we'll see next," added Jasmine. "There are so many places that need our help."

Ellie took the emerald out of her pocket. "We need a really safe place to keep this."

"If only there was room in the Magic Box," said Summer.

The lid of the box opened as if it had heard her. There was no space for it alongside all their magical treasures. But suddenly the top tray floated up in the air. Underneath were four empty compartments!

"Perfect!" said Ellie as she slotted the emerald into the first space. "Nobody will find it there."

The tray of treasures flew into place again, then the Magic Box closed.

The girls exchanged a small smile. "We've got a lot more work to do," said Jasmine. "But at least we've started making things right again."

The three friends hugged each other. They couldn't wait to go back and save the Secret Kingdom!

Join Ellie, Summer and Jasmine
in the next Secret Kingdom
adventure,

Sapphire Spell

Read on for a sneak peek...

Summer's Birthday

Summer Hammond stood very still and
held out a handful of animal food. The
two deer came close to the fence and
snuffled at her hand. Their eyes were like
forest pools – deep and dark. Summer
grinned as she reached out and stroked
their velvety noses. She thought they
were beautiful – but then she loved all

animals, even spiders!

"Smile!" Jasmine called out from behind her.

Summer turned and grinned as Jasmine quickly took a couple of photos.

"Don't move for a second!" Ellie called from where she was crouching down on the grass, drawing a quick picture of the deer in her notebook. She loved to draw and always carried a notebook and pen around with her. She drew a few more lines and then carefully tore the page out. "Happy Birthday!" she said, offering it to Summer.

Summer gave the deer one last pat and went over to see the drawing. It was brilliant. It completely captured the gorgeous animals, and her huge grin! "Thank you!" Summer hugged Ellie.

"This is just the best way to spend my birthday – at Honeyvale Wildlife Park with my two best friends and lots of animals!" she declared.

They all smiled at each other.

"I love it here," said Jasmine. "All the different animals give me ideas for dance steps. Look, this is how a squirrel moves…" She ran with short light steps and hid behind a tree, popping her head out. "And this is a deer." She leaped into the air, throwing her head and arms back.

Ellie stuffed her notebook in her backpack and grinned. "And this is a rabbit!" She crouched down and did some bunny hops before tripping over a tree root and landing on her tummy.

"A very clumsy rabbit!" Summer

giggled. The deer skittered away, bounding gracefully into the trees.

Their movement stirred a memory in Summer's mind. "Do you remember the magic reindeer we met in the Secret Kingdom?" she said to her friends. "They were even more beautiful than these deer."

"Oh yes," said Ellie. "And they could fly!"

The Secret Kingdom was an amazing land that only they knew about. It was a beautiful place that was usually ruled by kind, jolly King Merry. But recently something terrible had happened – his horrible sister, evil Queen Malice, had taken over! She had built a bridge into the troll territories, and the trolls had helped her steal King Merry's crown and put him in a dungeon. The queen had declared herself the ruler of the Secret Kingdom and now everyone there had to do whatever she said.

"I wonder how King Merry is," Summer said anxiously.

Jasmine frowned. "I hate thinking of him being locked away in Thunder Castle."

"And everyone in the Secret Kingdom being so unhappy because of Queen Malice and the trolls," said Ellie. "Oh, I hope we can find the missing jewels!"

Read

Sapphire Spell

to find out what happens next!

Have you read all the books in Series Five?

Queen Malice has taken over the Secret Kingdom! Can Ellie, Summer and Jasmine find all the royal jewels and make King Merry rule again?

Catch up on the very first Secret Kingdom adventures in this beautiful treasury!

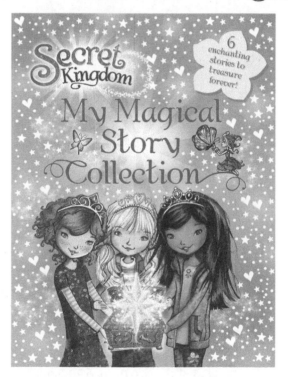

With gorgeous colour illustrations!

Available
September 2014

Look out for the next sparkling special!

Join the girls on a special starry adventure!

Available
October 2014

Code Breaker

King Merry needs your help! Can you break the code to help him remember what he's lost?

A B C D E F G H I
J K L M N O P Q R
S T U V W X Y Z

_ _ _   _ _ _ _ _

Competition!

Queen Malice's trolls might be big and mean, but they have a secret talent. All trolls love to sing...badly!

One of the trolls' musical notes is hidden somewhere in the pages of every Secret Kingdom book in series five.

Did you spot the note when you were reading this book?

Help Summer, Jasmine and Ellie stop the terrible noise!

Enter the competition by finding all four hidden notes and entering the page numbers at

www.secretkingdombooks.com

We will put all of the correct entries into a draw and select one winner to receive a special Secret Kingdom goodie bag featuring lots of sparkly gifts, including a glittery t-shirt!

Good luck!

A magical world of
friendship and fun!

Join the Secret Kingdom Club at

www.secretkingdombooks.com

and enjoy games, sneak peeks and lots more!

You'll find great activities, competitions, stories
and games, plus a special newsletter for
Secret Kingdom friends!